Can I Have Some?

"Can I have some?" said Milly.

"No, not yet!" said Max.

"Put on the nose," said Mom.

"There," said Max.

"Can I have some?" said Dad.

"No, not yet!" said Mom.

"Put on the mouth," said Mom.

"There," said Max.

"Can we have some now?"
said Dad and Milly.

"No, but come on in,"
said Mom.